Grandma in the Stars

Sneha Sharma

Ukiyoto Publishing

All global publishing rights are held by

Ukiyoto Publishing

Published in 2023

Content Copyright © Sneha Sharma

ISBN 9789360160364

All rights reserved.

No part of this publication may be reproduced, transmitted, or stored in a retrieval system, in any form by any means, electronic, mechanical, photocopying, recording or otherwise, without the prior permission of the publisher.

The moral rights of the author have been asserted.

This is a work of fiction. Names, characters, businesses, places, events, locales, and incidents are either the products of the author's imagination or used in a fictitious manner. Any resemblance to actual persons, living or dead, or actual events is purely coincidental.

This book is sold subject to the condition that it shall not by way of trade or otherwise, be lent, resold, hired out or otherwise circulated, without the publisher's prior consent, in any form of binding or cover other than that in which it is published.

www.ukiyoto.com

*To my maternal Grandfather
Hari Shankar Sharma,
who taught us to love and share stories.*

Acknowledgment

Sonia, my sister - for being the constant emotional pillar of my life.

My two loving families – for celebrating my every success – big or small.

My Nani-house in Nashik – for gifting memories of a lifetime.

My amazing children – Abir, for intently listening to all the stories I made up for you and encouraging the idea of crafting a book. Anhad, for eagerly waiting for the story to come out and being the sweetheart you are!

My husband, Sanskar Sharma – For being my wizard. Nothing I do or am exists separate from your and our children's presence.

Contents

Chapter 1	1
Chapter 2	5
Chapter 3	8
Chapter 4	17
Chapter 5	20
About the Author	*35*

Chapter 1

Ayesha closed her eyes and pictured the swing hanging from the Peepal tree. She imagined the vast fields and the adorable newborn calf of the white cow, Leela. Just as she was lost in her thoughts, Shreya teased her of daydreaming.

Shreya and Ayesha had already chosen a name for the calf – 'Chatur.'

Ayesha had lost her Nani-maa (Grandma) two years ago during a pandemic. Shreya knew that her best friend missed her Nani-maa more than anything, so she had convinced her to spend the summer vacation at her own Nani's house in Nashik.

The girls packed their bags with cheerful summer clothing in shades of pink and white and their favorite storybooks by Ruskin Bond and Enid Blyton. With their backpacks ready, they set off for their vacation. Living in Delhi, Ayesha had never experienced a village life firsthand, except through Shreya's vivid stories.

The large iron gate creaked open, welcoming the two girls to Shreya's Nani's old bungalow. Shreya's Mamaji stood near a beautiful white cow, Leela, who was contentedly chewing her cud in the morning sunlight. As Mamaji spotted their car, he set down the two buckets filled with freshly churned cow's milk. Ayesha instantly recognized Leela and waved at her as the car was smoothly parked in the cattle shed.

Ayesha was delighted to meet everyone. Shreya's Nani-maa, who was in a wheelchair and couldn't speak much, looked elderly, even more so than Ayesha's own Nani. Nevertheless, she was charming and offered Ayesha a Tulsi leaf after completing her pooja. However, Ayesha couldn't wait to meet Chatur.

Mamaji led the two friends to a small, dimly lit room beneath Leela's shed, where the little wonder was napping on the greenish-yellow hay. They were instructed not to disturb him, as he might wake up and rush to his mother for milk, interrupting her peaceful lunch.

The playful little calf was quick enough to make the two girls fall in love with him. He was everything Ayesha had heard about through her best friend. The mother seemed relieved to see her calf being baby-sat and how!

Far away from her own home, Ayesha found herself playing in the vast backyard open to the sky of Shreya's house in this small village of Maharashtra. There was usually no electricity in the evenings. The authorities cut it to save power, but Ayesha was in no mood for a spoiler! She was ecstatic, which meant she was pleased, as she had the best companions in Shreya and Chatur!

A few minutes later, *Mamiji* called them to sleep.

"Shreya! Ayesha! Bedtime! Come to the terrace!!"

"Terrace?" Ayesha inquired.

"When there's no electricity at night, we sleep on the terrace!"

"How is that?"

"Come with me." Shreya held Ayesha's hand and charged up the stairs.

A trillion stars twinkled quietly in the universe while the wind hummed the night song to the full moon – bright and charming!

Ayesha twirled around as the frills of her dress swayed in joy. She had never seen such a beautiful night sky. Awe-struck, she stumbled upon a pillow on the floor and noticed the beds neatly arranged in a row.

"We'll be sleeping here tonight!" declared *Mamiji*.

"All of us?"

Mamiji nodded confidently.

"Yay!" whooped Ayesha and ran across the terrace in delight, pausing momentarily to admire the moonlit sight of Chatur nestled in his mother's warmth, sleeping like an angel. She then gazed at the stars and couldn't help but miss her Nani-maa. She would have been with Ayesha this time of the year if she were still alive.

Shreya marveled at her friend and found it amusing how she was excited about everything she saw in the village. But she was glad that Ayesha didn't seem to miss her Nani as much. With that thought, Shreya drifted into a deep slumber.

But Ayesha was enchanted by the night, and so enchanted was she that she couldn't sleep.

Chapter 2

Just then, in the tranquil silence of the moonlit night, she heard a gentle rap on the door. Ayesha glanced around, her eyes shifting left and right. Most of the people in the house were asleep on the terrace.

"Who could it be then?" she whispered, feeling a bit anxious.

Shreya was snoring away, unlikely to wake anytime soon. With slow and nervous steps, Ayesha approached the door and opened it cautiously.

To her surprise, it was Chatur! He excitedly pushed his way in, glancing at Ayesha with his broad, deep eyes.

"Hi, Ayesha!"

"Chatur! You can talk!"

"Mmm..hmm..and I know you find me cute!"

"Shreya! Wake up!" Ayesha muttered, nudging the snoring Shreya with her foot.

"Psst psst..don't waste time, girl, come with me!"

"And where are we going?"

"Into the fields! My friend over there is waiting for us."

Ayesha grasped the lantern, and together, they descended the stairs, entering the courtyard. The path was lined up with grass and peculiar flowers. The moon and the dark sky turned everything inky blue! The flowers towered above the grass, like naughty children in a classroom, eager to glimpse the newcomer passing by.

Perched high on a branch was a black cat, its shiny eyes resembling small, colorful glass marbles, ready to engage in nighttime chatter with the moon.

"Isn't the breeze lovely?" Ayesha remarked.

"You're welcome!" said Chatur, pointing his nose towards the sky.

"But I didn't thank you," Ayesha said.

"You're in my village now. The trees here also belong to my village, so you're welcome," Chatur retorted.

"Well, thanks to the wise men who planted these trees."

"Well, they, too, belong to my village. So, you're welcome!"

"Oh really? You're starting to sound just like my little brother, an annoying little man!" Ayesha teased. Their playful banter gradually gave way to a muddled conversation. Eventually, the gentle wind sang a soothing lullaby to the flowers, coaxing them to sleep once more as the night's entertainment had ended.

Chapter 3

"Ah! There he is!" Chatur exclaimed.

"He who?" Ayesha squinted into the open field.

"Ratan," Chatur replied.

"Ratan? I can only see a scarecrow... and wait, he's moving!"

"That's him!" Chatur eagerly bounded in the direction of Ratan, the living scarecrow.

"Welcome to the fields, Ayesha! How have you been? Why do you look so surprised? Didn't Shreya ever tell you about me?" Ratan appeared taken aback by Ayesha's bewildered expression. He was a tall, straw-haired man—well, more accurately, a scarecrow—wearing a white dhoti and kurta. Without his clear and hearty voice, one would never have guessed his true nature.

"Because I suppose..." Ratan continued introducing himself, "...for Shreya, I'm just a scarecrow. Her grandmother knows the secret, so she never lets Shreya come to me, especially at night!"

"What... secret!?" A petrified Ayesha inquired.

"That this splendid friend is no ordinary scarecrow, don't be afraid. He's just having a bit of fun. He's going to help us on our journey." Chatur chimed in reassuringly.

"Let's hop on his shoulders; we must use the night before it is spent."

With that, Ratan dashed forward, seeming to meld with the wind, while Ayesha and Chatur clung to his shoulders. Ayesha felt her stomach drop, and the wild wind filled and dried her mouth so fiercely that she couldn't close it, making her lips dance in a frenzied disco.

The trio arrived near an old cottage with a solitary window, where Ratan gently set down his two passengers.

10 Grandma in the Stars

"Let's maintain a two-foot distance from this cottage and chant the incantation," Ratan urged, unloading his passengers.

"Incantation?" Ayesha inquired, her curiosity piqued.

"Ahem... well, you see, in my free time, I like to pick up books, and I came across the word 'incantation' in Mark Twain's Tom Sawyer when Tom and his friend sing this magic spell..." Ratan said, a touch of pride in his voice before Chatur interjected.

"He simply means a magic spell," Chatur clarified.

"But wait!" said Ratan. "We must tell Ayesha about Bheema."

"Alright, Ayesha, pay attention," Chatur began, conjuring an image for Ayesha. "We're about to open a window to the ferocious wind."

"Well, that's not a wind; that's a snore." Ratan punctured the thought balloon Ayesha had just begun to blow.

"You two are scaring me off! Let's go back to the terrace!" Ayesha said.

"Okay, let me explain," Chatur took charge. "Bheema the bull rests in this special cottage."

"Past midnight, he lets out a massive snore on full moon nights," Ratan added.

"We are going to take Ratan's shoulders as launch pads, and as we open the window, the snore shall catapult us straight..into…the…stars!" Chatur concluded with a triumphant raise of an eyebrow.

Ratan spoke like a wise older brother, advising them, "But remember to come back before the powerful yellow-faced guardian of the sky awakens!"

"The sun! We know, baba!!" Chatur reassured.

Ayesha watched, bewildered, as Chatur and Ratan, like two ace wizards, took turns to spell the magic.

"Time has come

To take us there

The magic begins

So don't be square!"

They cautiously opened the window with a nervous gulp and swiftly shut it with equal speed.

"What's going on?" Ayesha asked, startled and already overwhelmed by the night's unexpected events.

"He's awake!" Ratan warned, clearly exhausted from the strenuous task of opening Bheema's window.

"Did he see you guys?" Ayesha asked.

"No! Thank goodness! Ayesha, we got to put him to sleep! Anyhoo!!" Chatur commanded.

"So, what's the plan?" Ratan inquired, his mind racing to devise an idea to lull Bheema to sleep.

"I can sing a lullaby... uuuuwwwaahhhh!" Ayesha began to sing, but Ratan quickly placed his stick-like finger over her lips, gesturing for her to be quiet.

"Wait!! Have you lost your mind, girl? This bovine in there is dangerous! He is not a baby who...."

"Wait... it's unusual for Bheema to stay up so late," Chatur chimed in before Ratan could finish his sentence, sounding like Detective Karamchand. "Usually, by this time, he's fast asleep. I think something is bothering him. I'll need to open the window and peek inside."

"It's the fly! Hovering over that poor thing..!" exclaimed Ratan.

"Oh, so it's Champa! 'The Nomad of the Farm'!!" Chatur confirmed.

"Ain't any ordinary insect! She puffs up in epic proportions and transforms into a giant fly! And then – she makes a huge trash bin appear out of thin air and unleashes it on anyone who looks like they want to mess with her!"

"And the stench isn't just a bit worse than the garbage we toss in our waste bin, blaarrgh!! No, it's way, way worse!" Ratan painted a vivid picture.

"That's disgusting!" said Ayesha.

"Yup..and it's usually Bheema's dung!" Chatur added matter-of-factly.

"Eeeewwwww!" the three of them chorused.

"I have an idea." Ayesha produced a lollipop and hid behind the side wall near the window. Ratan tore its wrapper, and Champa zoomed out of the window with a loud buzz, making a sharp turn right toward the alluring, round, orange ball on a stick Ayesha was holding out.

"Mmm….yummy…delicious…scrumptious…"
Champa muttered, desperately trying to wedge her dirt-covered dancing feet into the solid surface of the lollipop, savoring its sugary orange flavor.

"Bheema is asleep!!" Chatur whispered in an excited tone but felt a tickling on his back.

"Oh dear, dear! Let me have some fun with my muse, won't you?" Champa replied with a menacing look.

"But why won't you let Bheema sleep?" inquired Chatur.

"Because this place, my dearie, was once my home! My clan and I used to sit here for hours together and feast on this ground, which used to be adorned with dirt jewels! Oh dear, I feel so nostalgic! And your beloved

'Mama-ji' turned it into this stupid cottage for that heavy, dim-witted bovine!" sniffed Champa.

"I am not avenged yet," Champa added firmly.

"But you usually come in the evening. Why this time?" asked Ratan, who knew her routine.

"Oh dear! I was passing by, so I thought I'd have some fun!"

"Hey!! Stop wiping your dirty feet on me, you litterbug!" said Chatur, utterly disgusted.

"Oh yeah? Let me in, or else you'll have no choice!"

"Let me handle this," Ayesha stepped forward confidently to deal with the stubborn insect. "Hi, I am Ayesha!" she greeted the fly.

"Whatever!" Champa said.

"Could you please let Bheema's snores launch us into the stars?"

"Bhoo..bhoooo..hhuu hhahaha!!" Champa sniggered and burst into uncontrollable laughter.

"Shhhh…you are going to wake him up!" Ratan said.

"Which fool among these two told you such nonsense about Bheema? That idiot bull can only toil in the farms, release massive poo, and eat like a giant, but launching someone in the stars? Ha! That's nothing short of wild imagination!" said Champa.

"Ayesha, don't listen to her, she's…" Ratan began to say something but was interrupted by something unbelievable.

"Whoa!!" The three friends shouted.

Champa had ballooned into a gigantic fly, summoning a bucket out of thin air and directing it to her target – the three innocent onlookers standing on the ground, watching her in terror.

"Blaargh!!" The three nearly vomited from the overpowering stench of the bucket filled with nauseating litter. At that moment, another brilliant idea struck Ayesha like a lightning bolt.

"Wait! I have a deal! Can't we arrange a delicious meal for you and maybe introduce you to an extraordinary dump land or something after our journey so you would let us go now?"

"Hmmm..sounds fun! What's the deal?" Suddenly, the bucket vanished, and the size of the fly became humble again.

"Well, for now, I only have these…"

Ayesha revealed colorful *'laddoos'* and *'patashas'* from her pocket and extended her arm. *Mamiji* had given them to her in the evening to snack on.

"Oh, dear! Irresistible!" Champa buzzed excitedly around the soft laddos and instantly disappeared into them. Ayesha carefully placed the *laddoos* and the housefly on a *'choupal'* attached to the Peepal tree beside the swing.

While they waited for Bheema's snoring, Ayesha pulled out an old picture of her Nani-maa from her pocket. In the photo, they both had sweet *'aam-ras'* mustaches, with their tongues licking their lips. Ayesha felt a deep yearning for her grandma, and her eyes welled up with tears of sorrow.

Chapter 4

Just then, Champa noticed Ayesha's tears gleaming in the moonlight.

"Who's she?" Champa said, peering at a sepia-toned photograph in Ayesha's hands.

"My Nani-maa. She's somewhere up in those stars now. But I miss her."

"Is that why you want to go up into the stars?"

"Yeah! I might find her there and at least say my final goodbye," Ayesha paused, her face brightening, "Or even better, perhaps bring her back with me?"

"Back to Earth?"

"To her home, to Mom, and me!"

"I don't know if that's possible. Nobody who has ever left Earth in a real way, without those flying machines and all, has ever returned. But..you might get lucky!"

Champa remembered her clan – feasting and frolicking. Ayesha's longing touched Champa's heart.

She flew straight into Bheema's cottage and closed the curtains from inside to block out the moonlight. Her actions were a bit puzzling, but it seemed as if she was humming a tune of bee music, buzzing in between to catch her breath.

Champa then took out a magic spray from her magical bucket, which smelled like Jasmine, and sprayed it around the room, creating a barrier to keep the mosquitoes at bay and dimming the '*jugnoos*,' the excited tiny fireflies, who had turned Bheema's room into a movie theatre. Well, what with the whole crazy affair unfolding in the dingy cottage, the show wasn't any less exciting than a Rajnikant movie!

Finally, Bheema fell into a deep slumber and was about to start snoring when Champa whispered with excitement to the trio through the window –

"When Chapma can spread litter, she can spread fragrance too. Get going, you guys! Launch yourself into the endless night sky…the stars are waiting for you!"

Her voice trailed off, but it would linger in Ayesha's ears throughout her chilly journey to the stars and for a long time afterward.

"Woo hoo!" whooped the trio, and the massive snore propelled them skyward like a space rocket, soaring into the vast universe with Ratan's shoulders as their launchpads.

Ayesha lost her hairband and one shoe to the wind, but it didn't matter now. Chatur offered her his back to sit on, although he couldn't keep his four legs and ears straight; the wind forced them to bend backward, and his eyes closed while his lips danced. But they defied the strong wind and headed straight for their destination... into the village of the beautiful night sky!

Chapter 5

"Why is everything so blurry here? Is it fog?" Ayesha got down from Chatur's back and spoke mesmerized.

"That's because you are blocking my flashlight!" said a voice from behind.

Both turned toward it in surprise.

A stout, round man with a grey hat and a smile so wide he could eat a banana sideways greeted them with his hands on his waist.

"You're the moon, aren't you? You..are.. so beautiful!" Ayesha said.

"Thanks! But I don't work by compliments. Lady, I'll still have to check your gadgets!"

"We don't have any!" answered Chatur.

"And I am not allowed to have any!" Ayesha gasped.

"Good for you, young lady, because I can't let you enter with those electricity-consuming devices stuffed in your pockets. All I'm concerned about is my electricity bills! It piles up too many Moonpies, you see that I must pay to the Bossy-pants. You know, I get all my power supply from the irritable owner of this place? By the way, be cautious around him and leave before he yawns and snaps out of his drowsiness!"

"The Sun?" Ayesha and Chatur exclaimed in chorus.

"Yup! He's the boss around here. You're lucky we have a free entry here because A – you come from The Big sister's house – The Earth, and B – it's the holiday season at Moontown - the place where the sky's the limit, literally! Moon said, pointing towards the banner beneath the neon light that read 'Moontown.'

"The Lunar Eclipse is around the corner. I'll go for hibernation, while The Big sister and Bossy Pant will face off and sort some issues out. I guess it's the Earth's spinning that makes Bossy dizzy."

"By the way, I'm glad you didn't arrive in a space rocket. Those big ones gobble up too much of my electricity to charge. Although, I think this little guy here is just starting to learn his moon-landing chops!"

The moon chuckled as he affectionately stroked Chatur behind his ears.

Chatur secretly made a face and felt slightly offended but gulped his anger down.

"The town has been named after me, but all I am is just a tiny satellite, moving round and round the bigger planet."

Amid their conversation, a delightful scent of flowers wafted in from the entrance.

"You came through Bheema if I am not wrong!" said a voice from behind. It was Heena, a tiny glittering, fluttering fairy spraying an *'itra'* or perfume made of marigold and rose petals, which was simply enchanting.

Chatur took a deep whiff and exclaimed, "Moon-town smells wonderful!"

Out of the torchlight, Ayesha felt she was in a vast vacuum of darkness as she looked around, but it wasn't scary at all! She gazed into the distance and realized there was something brilliantly shiny deep within the vast darkness.

The fairy pointed towards that shiny, distant thing.

"That's the Milky Way, my friends!! Trillions of stars in it are homes to people who have ever been loved when they were alive!"

'I knew it; people live on even after they die!' the thought made Ayesha's eyes twinkle. She gazed into the distance, towards the Milky Way.

"Grandma, I am coming right away!" She exclaimed.

"Just how many zeros are there in a trillion?" Chatur wondered aloud as both friends hopped onto the fairy's back. They had just realized they had become as tiny and shiny as the fairy herself!

"This white carpet is so beautiful!"

Ayesha had just landed at an entrance, streaming her way on the fairy's back with Chatur, through the trillion chattering stars of the milky-way, into the Moon-town, where the dazzling light around her made her feel like a Bollywood star at an award ceremony.

"That's stardust," the fairy twinkled.

Ayesha removed the single shoe on her foot to feel the stardust beneath her toes. But as she strode forward, her steps felt light, as if she were gliding. She couldn't help but giggle at the feeling of being so weightless and agile. She took large, bounding strides that gracefully carried her across the lunar landscape, and Chatur was gliding along her side!

"It looks like white sand, but it's incredibly soft to touch, like baby powder!" she exclaimed. "And look at them..the people there! They have wings and the brightest smiles!"

"So, it's the dental bling that shines, not the stars," said Chatur.

"Have you been here before?"

"Yeah, once, right after I discovered my powers. I've always wanted to meet the clown who lives in the Moontown. Mom said he swings on a big swing and eats bananas all the time. He gifts children a magic lozenge that makes us giggle! But I guess Mom was making it up because when I arrived here, it was already morning. I only saw the Sun turning in his giant bed and reaching for the alarm by the bedside; I got terrified and tumbled back down to my shed."

But a curious Ayesha was lost in her surroundings, seeing people looking like tiny white humans with wings.

"What are these guys doing?" Ayesha inquired.

"They're all doing what they had enjoyed doing most when they were alive," the fairy spoke gently.

Ayesha closely observed the little white beings. They resembled statues made from plaster of Paris, brought to life, smooth and bluish-white, their heads huddled together in groups over activities Ayesha could recognize, were from Earth! The people were half her size and engrossed in the activities, just like children at a summer camp. Some were playing Sweep, the fun card and number game she used to play with her father. Others were absorbed in the game of Chess, hardly bothering to lift their heads to acknowledge the visitors in their town. Some were even playing with their dogs, which made Ayesha chuckle. However, her laughter faded when she spotted a massive figure, larger than she and Chatur put together, vertically and horizontally, snoring like a giant!

The guide fairy chuckled, her voice filled with amusement. "Meet Kumbhakarana, who's been snoozing for a long time. But you know what? Kids can't resist bouncing on him, so he's got a super special ticket to Moon-town!"

"Dental floss, dental floss, anyone?" came a voice from behind, ringing a bicycle bell.

"Hey, it's our milkman, Chaman Pyare!" Ayesha exclaimed with excitement.

"Hi, Ayesha, how are you? Welcome to the Moontown, where dreams come true!" greeted Chaman Pyare.

"Literally!" chorused the friends.

"I'm good! It's great to see you, Pyare bhaiyya! What's this new thing you're up to?"

"I've always enjoyed selling things to people, you know, ever since I was a kid. I even once sold my grandfather's old dentures to kids who wanted to prank their neighbors. I used to craft rabbits from the fallen leaves of the Arjun tree near our old school and sold them to my classmates. And now, after becoming a citizen of this beautiful place, I'm selling dental floss to the people of Moontown. It's like a magical blend of salt and stardust!" The salesman whispered the last part into Ayesha's ear. "You know how they love to smile and laugh all the time," added Chaman Pyare, showing off his dazzling incisors.

.---.....

Ayesha saw a narrow lane lined up with tiny houses on both sides, with roofs covered in sparkling frost and windows lit with lamps burning inside them. Strolling along the path, she noticed a small house set apart from the row of cottages that stretched from one end to the other.

The house was nestled within a cozy hedge decorated with crystal orchids and astral roses. These unique flowers had see-through, crystal-like petals that played with the gentle lantern light from the cottage, creating enchanting patterns of color and shine.

She gently tapped on the door as Chatur looked on curiously.

""Hi there! I'm Ayesha! May I come in?" she asked.

An elderly lady with a long nose, wearing a snug little woolen cap, appeared at the door. She looked like a hornbill in bathroom slippers.

But her eyes were kind.

"Oh, hello there! Guests from Aunt Earth, I'm Nimmi. And guess what? I spotted this fellow hiding behind the Moon's wardrobe when the Sun woke. Hahaha! You were frightened, weren't you?" She began talking as soon as she opened the door.

"Looks like an ordinary calf, but he's a wunderkind! Never mind. You, my lovely lady, come right in!" the old lady continued as the duo finally entered the house.

"This place is absolutely enchanting!" Ayesha exclaimed, taking in the house filled with fragrant jasmine and lily flowers. A window offered a view of a pond, which appeared almost magical as it sparkled in the sunlight. A pristine white lotus graced the pond's surface, smiling kindly as Ayesha gazed at it.

"Life here is so peaceful. At my age, all a lady desires is peace. Speaking of age, well, I may be getting on in years, but I'm still full of energy," the old woman chuckled.

"And quite beautiful, too! So, have you seen her?" Ayesha extended a photo of her grandmother.

"Oh! So, YOU are Tara's granddaughter, Ayesha?" The old lady examined the photograph, flashed a mysterious smile, looked at Ayesha, and then back at the picture.

"Yes, my Nani's name is Tara," Ayesha said, turning to Chatur, her confusion evident, and then back to the old lady.

"Over there!" She pointed toward an older woman through the open window, gracefully gliding in a pink cotton sari adorned with beautiful white flower patterns. She was accompanied by a wonderfully white and grey creature, carrying her and several other children.

"Doesn't it look like the Himalayan fish, the golden Mahaseer? I have seen its pictures in Shreya's encyclopedia that she sometimes reads under the shed! Only this one has wings in place where there should have been fins." quipped Chatur.

But Ayesha's eyes were glued to her Nani-maa, who looked like an Indian version of Cinderella's fairy godmother. The children clinging to her waist as they rode on the mysterious bird were all whooping in excitement.

"That's Sundari, our Airbus lady, kind enough to give free bus rides to these children daily," said Nimmi, the old lady resembling a hornbill. "And the lady you see on it is the Santa of the stars!" "She tells us so many stories about you, Ayesha!"

Ayesha shouted, "Nani-maa!" and rushed out of the door. She lost her balance and tumbled while trying to stop the flying bus. Sundari, the bus lady, glided to a halt. Tara descended from her ride gracefully, like a majestic queen dismounting from her stallion in the night sky. Silvery glitters trailed from the corner of her pallu as she stood facing Ayesha.

Nani-maa was overwhelmed with joy. It was only when Ayesha rushed over to give her a hug that she realized who was there.

"Nani-maa, you look so magical!"

"Ayesha! I never thought I would see you again!" Nani-maa replied.

"Chatur brought me here!"

"My pretty Ayeshu, your hair has grown so long! And you've started looking just like your Mom!" Tara said in absolute amazement, gently running her fingers through Ayesha's fine hair.

She signaled to a tiny cloud lazily floating in the night sky like a puppy taking a nap. Immediately, it lowered a swing made from the cloud matter itself, adorned with sparkling stardust, for both the ladies to rest on.

"Do you remember how I tied your hair into four braids?" Tara reminisced about the old days.

"Yeah! My head looked like a bustling crossroad from above!" Ayesha replied with a nostalgic smile.

"And how I loved making *loungi ka achaar* for you."

"Even if I demanded for the *achaar* in the middle of the night! *Nani*, you're amazing!"

"Summers were when you wouldn't do anything without your Nani by your side! Those days on Earth were so different and so real, Ayesha."

"But it's summer again, Nani, and I am here with you."

"And for that reason, I can't express my happiness. You know, the mangoes from your Mama's farm have been calling out for a while now – 'Where's your little

Ayesha, Nani? We've been hanging upside down on the trees like *Betaal*...rescue us into a shake, won't you!'" Nani playfully mimicked the mangoes, sensing Ayesha's nostalgia, and they both shared a hearty laugh.

Nani sprinkled a pinch of stardust into the air, and out of nowhere, a plate of ripe mangoes appeared in her hand.

"Oh, your friend Gayatri's Dadu was about to come here. So, I asked him to pick a few good mangoes from Ballu's farm for my *gudiya rani*. I had this feeling that I'll be seeing you again! Here they are, all yours. Enjoy them with Chatur and Shreya!"

"But who's Ballu?"

"Your Mama-ji, that crazy one! Did you forget I call him Ballu out of love?"

"*Nani*, can you not come with us back home?"

"I can't, *beta*. I have to be with THEM!" Ayesha saw the white light dimming around her, and a soft spotlight slowly fell upon the kids, who looked like angels decorating their tiny houses with fairy lights.

"Who are those kids, Nani? They look so tiny and amazing!"

"They are special children, Ayesha. God missed them so much that He called them back as soon as they touched the earth."

"They never miss a day of gliding games with their beloved Tara. Oh, how they enjoy the 'Happy Wheels' and the 'Humpty's Fall' on Sundari's back!" quipped

Nimmi, who had been observing the joyful reunion of two kindred spirits with eager eyes.

Ayesha pondered – "But I miss you, Nani."

"My lovely Ayeshu, take this with you," Tara placed a small, glowing fairy light in Ayesha's hand and clasped it reassuringly.

"It will light up when you hold it, and you will remember that your *Nani* is here for a reason."

"Oh, but I want to stay.."

"Come on, Ayesha!!" suddenly, Ayesha heard Chatur yell and saw the Sun come out of his bedroom, narrowing his eyebrows at her. He opened his mouth, and a harsh heat of light fell on her cheeks and forehead.

As Chatur hurried towards the exit, he suddenly tripped over something and fell headlong onto the floor. He turned to see that it was a banana peel! There was a massive stack of bananas piled beside a swing. On the swing, a tall man dressed in colorful clothing with a painted face was eating a banana and gazing admiringly at Chatur.

"The clown!" Chatur exclaimed. But Ayesha dragged him towards the gate. The joker rummaged his pocket, and suddenly, an object soared in their direction.

"It's the magic lozenge!" Chatur screamed in delight.

Before Ayesha could make sense of it all and even bid goodbye to her Nani, she found herself and Chatur shrieking in chorus. They were hurtling down the Moon-town. After a while, towards the exit, it felt like a gigantic, gentle parachute had suspended them. They began swaying like a leaf floating to the ground, their hearts fluttering like birds learning to fly. But then, after a while, the invisible parachute vanished, and they felt themselves plunging towards the Earth, like being pulled by a giant cosmic magnet. Stars whizzed by like dazzling fireflies, and the Moon above shrank in the distance, resembling a distant lantern on a dark path.

But Ayesha hasn't stopped giggling yet. The Sun followed her to the terrace. Blue Aparajita plants shone in the earthen pots lined up along the terrace boundary wall.

"Aaayiiish!! What has happened to you? Chatur is waiting for us! Wake up, won't you?"

Ayesha woke up, rubbing her eyes, and spotted Shreya. She couldn't wait to tell her where she and Chatur had gone last night. But, when she squinted her eyes and saw the shimmering Sun, she gasped in terror. Then, she stammered, "Wait, was that all just a dream?"

"What dream?" Shreya asked.

"I can't believe it was only a dream!" Ayesha muttered to herself in disbelief.

Ayesha felt a bit disappointed, but the thought of Chatur brought a smile to her face, and she jumped out of bed. Just as she reached to tie her tousled hair into a ponytail, she felt something tangled in it. She shook her head, and a fairy light fell onto the floor!

Ayesha held it in her palm, and it lit up softly against the bright summer sky.

"Your reason to stay is bigger than mine to bring you back, Nani!" Ayesha whispered to herself and quietly slipped the fairy light into her frilly frock's pocket. She sprinted down the stairs where her bestie awaited her, eager to play with the mysterious calf named Chatur.

------------------*****------------------

THE END

About the Author

Sneha Sharma

Dr. Sneha Sharma holds a PhD in Media Management and is a Professor of Media Communication at a renowned business school in Indore. She is also a writer, speaker, coach, and voice artist. Her stories have been published on various platforms, such as Times of India, Woman's Era, Womensweb, SheThePeople, and The Children's Magazine, to name a few. As a scriptwriter, her film 'Adrashya Nari,' won the silver award at the Hawaii International Film Festival and at the Film Fest of the Usha Pravin Gandhi College of Management. It was also screened at the prestigious Mumbai International Film Festival.

Reach out to the author at, *wordnama2020@gmail.com*

www.ingramcontent.com/pod-product-compliance
Lightning Source LLC
LaVergne TN
LVHW041642070526
838199LV00053B/3505